Emmi says, "Hi!"

Written by Keri Johnson Clark
Illustrated by Carlos Lemos

ISBN 978-1-61225-166-0

Published by Mirror Publishing
Milwaukee, WI 53214

Printed in the USA.

To Ethan and Emmi, the two most wonderful children anyone could ask for.
You make me laugh everyday and I'm so proud of both of you.
I love you more than words can say.

"Hi!" Emmi said from inside her crib down the hall.
"Hi", replied her brother, Ethan.

"Hi!" Emmi said again with a delightful little smile on her face. "Hi", replied her brother once again.

Emmi was always saying, "Hi", one of the few words she was able to say.

In the morning when she awoke, Emmi would say, "Hi!" with the enthusiasm that only a one year old could have. That was the start to her day.

"Hi," her mommy would say.
"Hi'" her daddy would say.
"Hi," her brother would say.

Cute as she was, Emmi was a mischievous little girl.
She got herself into all kinds of trouble.

She would climb on the coffee table and stand up in triumph, smack dab in the middle of the table.

She would pick up a crayon and put it in her mouth sneakily, looking at her mommy as if waiting for her to say, "No, no!"

She would pick up her little shoe and slowly place it near her mouth as if taking a bite of a cookie.

But when Mommy would catch her doing something she shouldn't, Emmi would look at her mommy with a smile from ear to ear and say, "Hiiiii!!!"

Ethan's friends would come over to play and Emmi would quickly greet them with a, "Hi!" as they entered the door. Ethan's friends would leave and Emmi would again say, "Hi!" with as much oomph as the first greeting.

When Emmi and her mommy walked around the supermarket, all that could be heard was, "Hi!"

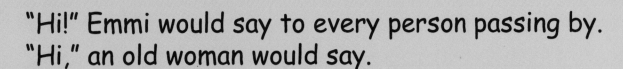

"Hi!" Emmi would say to every person passing by.
"Hi," an old woman would say.
"Hi," the gentleman picking out soup would say.
"Hi!" a toddler would say with the
  same amount of excitement
      as Emmi.

In line at the post office, Emmi would get fidgety and just couldn't stay still. That is, until she caught the eye of a little old lady with silvery white hair, waiting to buy stamps. "Hi", Emmi said to the little old lady.

"Hi. Aren't you adorable", the little old lady replied.
"Hi," Emmi would say again.
"Hi," the little old lady laughed. Emmi would say hi back and forth for hours if her mommy let her.

One night after dinner, Emmi was eating Jell-O. But instead of using her spoon, she reached into her pink little bowl, with her pudgy little hand and squished the Jell-O with all of her might.

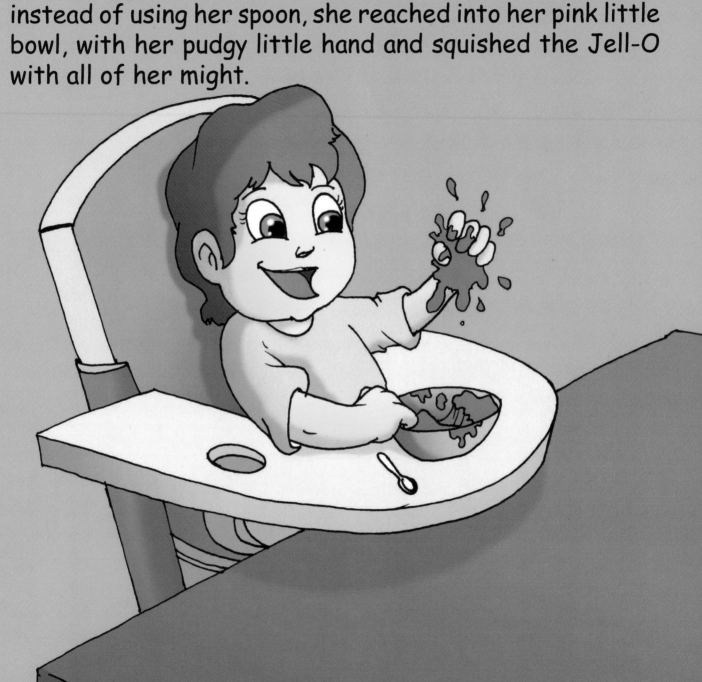

And as she squished that Jell-O, she looked right at Mommy and said, "Hiiiii!!"

She would say, "Hi!" to say hello and, "Hi!' to say goodbye. She'd say, "Hi!" to seek forgiveness and "Hi!" to get attention.

But one day, her gramma and grandpa were leaving the house. Everyone was hugging and saying goodbye.

"Bye" said Mommy. "Bye", said Gramma. "Bye" said Grandpa. "Bye" said Ethan.

"B-bye" said Emmi as she waved goodbye.